This Orchard book

belongs to

..........................................

# TEN LITTLE PIRATES

MIKE BROWNLOW  SIMON RICKERTY

ORCHARD

**Ten** little pirates, sailing out to sea,
Looking for adventure, happy as can be.
Are they hunting treasure? Are they going far?

**Ten** little pirates all say,
"**Arrrrrrr!**"

10

**Ten** little pirates and the weather's looking fine,

**Squawk!** goes an albatross – now there are . . .

. . . . nine

Nine little pirates,
searching for their mate.

9

# Zap!

goes the lightning –

now there are . . .

# ...eight.

**Eight little pirates, looking up to heaven.**

8

# Whoooosh!

goes a hurricane –

now there are . . .

· · · seven.

Seven little pirates,
really in a fix.

7

# Crash!

goes a great big wave – now there are . . . .

# ...five.

### Five little pirates spot a man-o'-war.

5

# BOOM!

goes a cannon –

now there are . . .

# "Coo-ee!"

calls a mermaid –

now there are . . .

# ...three.

Three little pirates, wondering what to do.

3

# Sploosh!

goes a water spout –

now there are . . .

# ...two.

Two little pirates, baking in the sun.

2

# Snap!

goes a hungry shark –

now there is . . .

# ...one.

One little pirate, sad and all alone,

No ship, no food, no way home.

1

Then **one**...

then **two**...

then **three**...

then **more!**

**All the other pirates splutter to the shore!**

Drinking milk from coconuts,
safe beneath a star,
Ten little pirates all say,

For my mother, Connie
M.B.

For Erin & Isla
S.R.

ORCHARD BOOKS
338 Euston Road
London NW1 3BH
*Orchard Books Australia*
Level 17/207 Kent Street, Sydney, NSW 2000

First published in 2013 by Orchard Books
First published in paperback in 2014
This edition published in 2014

ISBN 978 1 40833 694 6

Text © Mike Brownlow 2013
Illustrations © Simon Rickerty 2013

A CIP catalogue record for this book is available from the British Library.

1 3 5 7 9 10 8 6 4 2

Printed in China

Orchard Books is a division of Hachette Children's Books,
an Hachette UK company.
www.hachette.co.uk